D1316814

LITTLE SOUP'S BUNNY

LITTLE SOUP'S BUNNY

Robert Newton Peck

Illustrated by Charles Robinson

A YOUNG YEARLING BOOK

Published by
Dell Publishing
a division of
Bantam Doubleday Dell Publishing Group, Inc.
666 Fifth Avenue
New York, New York 10103

ISBN: 0-440-40772-9

Printed in the United States of America

March 1993

10 9 8 7 6 5 4 3 2 1

CWO

LITTLE SOUP'S BUNNY

One

Hi!
My name is Rob.
It's really Robert Newton Peck.
But my friends all call me Rob.
You can call me Rob too.
Why?
Because we are *pals*.

*   *   *

I grew up on a farm.
Our farm was in Vermont.
That's a state.
Not a big state like Alaska.
Vermont is small.
I was a lot smaller.
We Pecks were not rich people, but I always felt rich.
I'll tell you why.
Because I had a best friend.

His name was Luther Wesley Vinson.
His mother (for some odd reason) called him Luther, but I never did.
He didn't like it.

We kids called him Soup.
Even our teacher, Miss Kelly, called him Soup, whenever he was good.
She called him Soup about once a year.

— 2 —

I had a hunch that Miss Kelly silently called Soup a lot of things, but I never found out exactly what.

Soup lived on a farm too.
His farm was nearby, just up the road from our farm.
We were next-farm neighbors.
Best of all, we were *pals.*
We saw each other every day.
Seven days a week.

One April day Soup came to see me.
He wasn't running.
Soup was walking very slowly.
He was carrying something.
I couldn't see what it was, so I went up the dirt road to greet him.
I didn't walk.
I ran.

*   *   *

It's fun to run in April.

Do you know why?

Because the winter snow is now mostly puddles of water.

Cold water.

You have to run, and jump, then run more, and jump again.

I met Soup.

"Rob," he said, "look what I have."

I looked.

It was a baby rabbit.

Black and white.

"A bunny," I said.

Soup smiled.

"May I hold him?"

"Sure," he said, handing the bunny to me. "Please be gentle."

The baby rabbit was very soft.

* * *

"He's still a fawn," said Soup.

"His mother is a doe, and his father is a buck. Sort of like deer."

"I didn't know that," I said.

"Neither did I," said Soup.

"How did you find out?" I asked.

"I read it in a book."

Two

We walked toward my house.
Soup let me carry the baby bunny.
"Where did you get him?" I
asked.

"Aunt Clara brought him to me. He's my Easter reward for being a good boy for such a long time."

I laughed. "Okay," I said, "how long were you good?"

Soup grinned. "Almost an hour."

"What's your bunny's name?"

Soup shrugged.

"He never told me," he said.

Again I laughed.

It was super to have Soup for a pal.

His face was always smiling.

I smiled too.

It felt so good.

The rabbit fawn gave me a kick.

This bunny was little, but his kick felt quite big.

"Maybe he's hungry," I said.

We didn't go to my house.

Instead, we went to our vegetable shed.

Handing the baby bunny back to Soup, I opened the shed door.

It made a creaky sound, one that made my backbone feel chilly, even on a spring day.

We went inside.

All three of us.

In the shed it was dark and dry, but I liked how it smelled.

The smell was like a harvest.

We kept our vegetables and apples in the shed, until we ate them.

Most of our garden, however, got sliced up and canned by my mother, my aunts, my grandmother, and my four sisters.

"Never," Papa had warned me, "go into a kitchen where women are canning."

I reached into our carrot bin.

From a big brown burlap bag, I took out three orange carrots.

One for me.

One for Soup Vinson.

And one for the bunny.

We sat on a pair of apple barrels, outside in the April sunshine, and ate carrots.

There was a film of powdery earth on them, but nobody seemed to care.

*   *   *

To clean a carrot is easy.

You spit on it, and then wipe off the dirt on your pants. Or on somebody else's.

It's fun to bite a carrot.

For one thing, they never bite back.

For another, you hear a sharp *crack* as your teeth snap off a hunk.

"These are good," said Soup. "In fact, *your* carrots taste a lot like *ours*."

The bunny smelled his carrot.

His nose wiggled.

But he wouldn't bite it. Or eat it.

"I have an idea," said Soup.

"What is it?"

He handed the rabbit to me.

"Well," said Soup, "sometimes a baby

is too young to chew. But he's not too young to swallow."

Soup bit off a bite of carrot.
Then he chewed it.
But he didn't swallow any.
Instead, he took the chewed carrot out of his mouth and held it in his hand.
"Here," he told the bunny, "smell it again. Take another whack at it."

The bunny smelled it.
He nibbled it.
Then he swallowed.

Soup grinned.
"See," he said, "I'm sort of a mother rabbit."
"You mean you're a *doe*?"
Soup blinked.

"No, on second thought, I'm a buck, Rob, and so are you."

"But your bunny isn't a buck yet."

Soup grinned.

"No," he said, "he's a penny."

Three

"Easter is coming," Soup said.

"Yes," I said. "It's this Sunday."

"Right," said Soup.

The two of us were trying to climb a young maple tree, to reach an old bird's nest.

* * *

At first, I stood on Soup's shoulders. Then he stood on mine.

But we couldn't touch even the lowest branches.

The tree was too tall, and we were too short.

Soup's rabbit was there too.

Inside my shirt.

It's not easy to hold a pal up on your shoulders when a baby bunny is tickling your ribs with his fur.

I giggled, and Soup had to jump down.

"Rabbits don't climb trees," I said.

"No," said Soup, "they're not like cows."

I looked at Soup.

"*Cows* don't climb trees either."

Soup grinned. "I never said they did.

— 16 —

All I meant was that cows are something like rabbits."

I pointed. "Some are. Look."

Soup nodded. "Rob, you're right. He's black and white, like one of your Holstein cows."

"We still need a name for him."

"How about Cow?" Soup asked.

"A rabbit named *Cow*? You're nuts."

Soup made a face.

"Well," he said, "if Cow doesn't make any sense, how about Bull?"

Bulls are very big.

Soup's bunny was wee little.

"He doesn't look like a bull to me."

"Rob, he doesn't to me either."

"He looks closer to a bug."

Soup snapped his fingers.

— 17 —

"That's it! We can call him Buggy, because he's such a cute little bug."

I shook my head.
"What's wrong, Rob?"
"Buggy," I said, "just isn't right."
"How about Stinkbug?"
I laughed.
"He doesn't stink. Your little rabbit fawn smells sweeter than honey clover."
"Rob, is Beetle any better?"
"Not much," I said.
"How about Bowl Weevil?"

I looked at Soup. "What's that?"
"I heard my mother mention it. I think a weevil has something to do with specks that move in the dry cereal."
"Good," I said.
"Good? How come, Rob?"

"Because now," I told Soup, "if I don't eat my lumpy oatmeal, I can tell Mama there's a weevil in my bowl."

Soup sighed.

"By the time we think up a name for him, my bunny will be a grown-up buck."

"That's it," I said. "That's his name. Because he's only a baby buck."

"What is, Rob?"

I grinned. "Bucky."

Four

"Careful," said Soup.

We were at Soup's house.

Not *in* his house, but in his chicken coop, gathering eggs.

— 21 —

Bucky, the baby bunny, was asleep.
But this time inside Soup's shirt.

All babies take naps.
Babies, and my great-uncle Clarence.
He even sleeps in the bathtub.
Uncle Clarence didn't drown; but when he sank, his cigar sure went out.

"Easy does it," said Soup.
He was warning me not to drop an egg.
Soup was right.
A dropped egg isn't an egg any longer.

It's a sticky yellow goo.

"Soup, how many eggs do we have now?"

He looked in our basket.

"Ten. Eleven, counting the cracked one."

"That's enough."

"No, it isn't. Let's get ten more."

"Your mother may need fresh eggs for supper," I said, "so we'd best spare a dozen."

"Okay, Rob, okay."

Carrying the basket, and Bucky, we were leaving the hen yard.

"Where to?" I asked Soup.

"Out to the hay barn."

*   *   *

I almost tripped on a chicken.

"Watch it," said Soup. "Maybe you better let *me* carry the eggs."

"Okay." I handed him the basket.

"Rob," said Soup, "we need a bucket."

"For what?"

"To boil the water."

"You don't use a bucket to boil water."

"Well, we have to boil it in *something*."

"How do you know?" I asked.

"Rob, I watched my mother do it last Easter."

I nodded slowly. "Come to think of it, *my* mother did the very same thing. She boiled water."

"I don't know what for," said Soup.

"So let's not bother," I said. "We'll use plain old cold water."

We were now in the hay barn.

"And," said Soup, "here's our pot."

Five

Soup and I left the barn.

We went out to the brook in the cow pasture, carrying Bucky in a tin pot.

Then we gently dumped out Bucky in order to fill our pot with water.

Cold water.

*   *   *

We took off our shoes and socks and rolled up our pant legs, to keep our clothes dry.

My mother always told me to do this whenever I went near a brook.

She said that I could somehow get myself wet in a desert.

"Ah," said Soup, "that does it."

"What's the water for?" I asked.

"Coloring."

Reaching inside his pocket, Soup pulled out a collection of six tiny little bottles.

"What are those?" I asked.

"Vegetable dye."

"We're going to dye *vegetables*?"

"No," said Soup. "Rob, we are going to dye hen fruit. Eggs for Easter."

"Good idea."

*   *   *

Soup dripped a drop of green dye in the water, then used a twig to stir it.

"Ah," he said, "you're right. *We didn't need to boil the water.*"

"Where did you find the dye, Soup?"

"From my mother's pantry."

"Will she care?" I asked.

"Not until she misses it."

He stopped, pulling out the twig.

It had turned a bit green.

The dye was ready.

"Rob, hand me an egg."

I gave him one.

Soup laid an egg into the green water.

We waited.

Looking down into our pot, I could see the egg changing, from white to green.

"It's working, Rob."

"It sure is."

We dyed a second egg green.

Then we dumped out the green water, rinsed the pot in the brook, and filled it again.

"Now," said Soup, "for purple."

We dyed two purple eggs.

Then two red eggs.

Two blue eggs.

Two yellow.

And one orange.

The egg that was cracked.

Eleven in all.

Bucky wasn't much help.

He kicked over our last potful of orange water.

It spilled all over my bare foot.

* * *

"Look," I said, "my foot is orange all over."

Soup said, "Wash it off in the brook."

"Okay."

I dipped in the tip of a toe.

"Yikes," I said, "that water sure is cold."

Soup laughed.

"Maybe," he said, "it'll turn your foot blue."

I stopped.

"I'd rather keep it orange, for Easter," I told Soup. "At least the orange will cover up some of the dirt."

"And you won't have to take a bath before church."

"Right," I agreed.

Bucky hopped over, sniffed one of my orange toes, and then softly bit it.

"Rob," said Soup, "Bucky thinks your toe is a little carrot."

— 31 —

After putting our shoes and socks on, we left the brook and headed home.

"Wow," said Soup.

I had to say "Wow" too.

Our eleven eggs were a bouquet of April flowers.

"I can't wait for Easter," said Soup.

"Neither can I."

Thinking, I scratched my head.

"What will we do with our eggs?"

"I have a plan," said Soup.

"What kind of a plan? I've heard of an eggplant, but not an egg plan."

"We hide our eggs," said Soup.

"Why?"

"So," he said, "on Easter Sunday, we can ask our folks to guess where they are."

* * *

"Where can we hide them?"

Soup grinned. "Where eggs belong."

"Where's that?"

"In a nest."

Six

"Rob," said Soup, "we need one more thing."

I looked at Soup. "What's that?"

"A ladder."

The two of us were back at my house, holding our beautiful Easter eggs.

In six rainbow colors.

And trying to hold Bucky.

* * *

"Soup," I asked, "what does a ladder have to do with Easter Sunday?"

Soup smiled. "Nothing."

"Then why do we need a ladder?"

"Because we are both too little to climb a tree."

"Which tree?"

Soup pointed. "That one there."

He was pointing at the young maple tree we had earlier tried to climb.

As it was April, there were no leaves on the twigs.

But we couldn't climb it.

I looked up, up, up, up, up.

"Soup," I said, "that old bird's nest is sort of . . . high."

"All part of my plan, Rob."

"Will we get into trouble?"

"Of course not," said Soup.

*　*　*

Trouble! I said the word to myself.

Some of Soup's crazy ideas had a way of hatching.

Like a rotten egg.

"Now," said Soup, "let's get a ladder."

We went to our barn.

It took a while, but at last we found an apple ladder.

The ladder was very long.

Soup and I were very short.

So, as we carried the ladder, one long leg was up, while the other leg dragged.

A ladder has a lot of holes in it.

All of the holes are square.

Like windows.

"Holes won't weigh very much," Soup had said, "so it'll be a cinch to carry a ladder."

It wasn't easy.

A ladder isn't light.

It's heavy.

Holes and all.

The more square holes a ladder has, the heavier it is to carry.

It took plenty of pulling and dragging and tugging to bring the apple ladder to the tree.

Then we learned one thing more.

A ladder is not like a boy, or a rabbit, or a cow.

A ladder does not stand up by itself.

It takes a lot of work.

But we did it.

"Rob," said Soup, "the rest is easy."

"Easy as pie," I said.

I thought it would be.

But it wasn't.

To carry an egg in each hand, while balancing up a tall ladder, isn't hard.

It's impossible.

Soup tried to go first.

He took the two green eggs.

But then, halfway up, he almost dropped one of the eggs.

He had to climb down again.

Then I tried it.

I took a purple egg in each hand.

But I didn't make it to the top either.

"Perhaps," said Soup, trying to hold on to Bucky, "we ought to find a lower nest."

"Or," I said, "a shorter tree."

We needed a new hiding place for our eleven colorful Easter eggs.

And in our barn we found one.

A wooden shelf.

Better yet, there was an old basket on the shelf.

A big basket.

A bushel basket.

"It's all dusty," I said.

"Yes," said Soup, "but it's cleaner than we are."

We carefully placed our Easter eggs in our large brown Easter basket.

Then we hid the bushel basket on the shelf.

"I hope it doesn't fall," said Soup.

"Why would it?"

"Well," he said, "it's sort of too near the edge of that narrow shelf."

Looking up, I figured the shelf was close to seven feet up the wall.

Yet we had managed to reach it by climbing up some old barrels and boxes that sat underneath.

They were perfect for stairs.

Seven

It was night.
I was dreaming.
In my dream, I wasn't with Soup.
Instead, I was with . . . *her*.
Norma Jean Bissell.
She was the prettiest girl in our school.
Maybe in the whole world.

* * *

I didn't look at our teacher, Miss Kelly, a lot.

Instead, I looked at Norma Jean Bissell, until Norma Jean caught me doing it.

Then I'd quickly look at Miss Kelly.

I didn't want Norma Jean Bissell to know how much I liked her.

But she knew.

Because girls are different from boys.

Girls know more about *liking.*

Anyhow, in my dream, I was liking Norma Jean, and she was liking me. A lot!

She was saying my name. "Rob."
But something went wrong.
It wasn't Norma Jean's voice.
"Rob. Rob!"

My dream popped, like a busted balloon, and I opened one eye.

"Rob . . . wake up."
It was Soup's voice.
I stumbled to my bedroom window.
There he stood, down on the ground, hollering a whisper, and waving an arm.
"Hurry," he said. "Come on down."

I rubbed my eyes.
"It's the middle of the night," I told him.
"Rob, I need help."
"What's wrong?"
Soup's voice choked.
"Bucky's gone."

I put on a coat over my pajamas.
And one shoe.

I couldn't find the other one.

My other shoe is never around when I really need it.

Silently I crept down our dark stairs.

Soup was outside.

"Bucky's gone," he said again.

There were no tears in his eyes.

Only in his throat.

"Did somebody steal him, Soup?"

"No, I don't think so. It's my fault."

"How come?"

"I forgot to twist the lock latch on his hutch, and stick the peg in its loop."

"Maybe he kicked the door open."

Soup nodded.

"We have to find him," Soup said.

"Do your parents know you're up, out of bed, and away from home?"

Soup looked at his house.

"No, they don't. And I hope they won't."

"I bet *my* mother knows," I said. "Mama has a way of finding out everything."

Soup said, "Sort of like Miss Kelly."

Eight

It was dark.
Soup and I moved slowly.
We couldn't see too well.
The April moon had ducked behind a
cloud.
A big cloud.
I knew that Soup and I ought to

be asleep in our beds, instead of outside.

But we had to find Bucky.

The two of us yelled his name.
To yell in a whisper is not easy to do.
We couldn't make any noise.
Carefully we moved in the night.

My coat felt nice and warm.
One of my feet was warm too.
But the other one (my orange foot) was becoming quite cold.
Maybe, I was thinking, it really would turn blue!
In northern Vermont, an April midnight is *not* what you would call *hot weather*.
You might say *cold weather*.
Neighborly close to *winter*.

* * *

"Bucky," Soup whispered, "where are you?"

"Soup, did you look around up at your place before coming to get me?"

He nodded. "I looked, and called his name a lot. But he just wasn't anywhere."

"Maybe he's still in his hutch, down under all that straw."

"No," said Soup. "Bucky is gone. Why would he run away?"

It hit me!

"Soup, I know the reason."

He blinked at me in the dark.

"You do, Rob? Why?"

"Carrots."

Soup grinned.

"Of course. You're right, Rob. You gave Bucky his very first carrot."

We headed toward our shed.

* * *

"Miss Kelly was right," said Soup.

"About what?"

"Remember? She said that carrots give our eyes good eyesight."

"Yes," I said. "And something about rabbits too."

"What was it?"

"Well," I said, "as I recall, Miss Kelly said that rabbits sleep in the daytime and eat at night."

Soup looked at our vegetable shed.

"Ah," he said, "I bet that's where Bucky is."

"At the carrot bin."

In the daytime, our shed door creaks when you open it.

A soft little sound.

At night, however, the creak was louder.

And very spooky.
I felt cold.

My orange foot suddenly felt even colder.

"Hold it," I said through chattering teeth.

"Are you afraid, Rob?"

"No," I lied.

"Then why are you sitting down?"

"To take off my shoe, and put it on my orange foot."

"Why?"

"So my regular foot will be cold and turn blue. And I'll have a blue foot and an orange foot."

Soup sighed.

"And," he said, "an egg head."

Nine

Again I tried the door.

Its squeak sounded even louder.

Inside, there was no light to switch on.

Just inky blackness.

It made me wish that I'd eaten more carrots.

"Rob," said Soup, "you go in first."

"Why *me*?"

"It's *your* shed."

I stopped. "But," I said, "it's *your* bunny."

I didn't go first.

And neither did Soup.

We went together.

Very slowly.

One tiptoe step at a time.

One warm step (with my shoe foot) and then a cold step (with my bare foot).

"Bucky," whispered Soup.

"Where are you, Bucky?" I whispered.

We were whispering very softly.

Softer than a baby bunny.

I'll tell you why.

My rule is: Never make a lot of noise at midnight in a dark vegetable shed.

It gives me cold feet.

Or a cold foot.

Soup suddenly stopped.

"Rob, hear that?"

I listened. And heard a strange noise.

Soup's mouth was very close to my ear.

So close that he didn't really have to talk.

Only breathe.

"Rob, it sounds like . . . like teeth."

"Or," I said, "maybe *fangs.*"

"Vegetables don't have any teeth," said Soup.

"How do you know?"

He looked at me. "Have you ever seen a turnip at the dentist?"

But I still heard the noise.

As we moved forward, it grew louder.

My blue foot was freezing, and so were my heart and my blood.

"What is it, Soup?"

"Teeth," he said. "Somebody, or something, is maybe getting . . . eaten alive."

"Bucky?" I whispered.

"Oh, please," I heard Soup breathe. "Please don't let anything eat Bucky."

"Soup," I said, "I have an idea."

"What is it, Rob?"

"Help me open the main door."

We pulled together. The hinges creaked.

The moonlight streamed in through the doorway.

And then we saw it all.
Something *was* being eaten.
It was a carrot.
Eaten by Bucky.

Ten

I woke up.
And knew it was Sunday.
The sun came up too.
It looked as orange as my foot.
Outside, our rooster crowed, and my Easter morning cracked open like a fresh yellow egg.

* * *

First came chores.

If you live on a farm, you do for your animals before you do for yourself.

Next was breakfast.

I ate eggs.

To me, happiness is hearing my mother say those five welcome words: "We're all out of oatmeal."

Wearing our best clothes, some of which sported a few patches, we Pecks went to church.

In a wagon pulled by two horses.

Church lasted about twenty years.

And the brown wooden pew seemed to become harder every second.

The music was okay.

Except for Mrs. Stetson's solo, which

sounded like somebody trying to sharpen a dull saw with a rusty file.

She must have gargled with gravel.

As Sunday School members, Soup and I were prodded forward, and given large letters (on big squares) to hold up, for the grown-ups to see.

There were nine kids. And nine letters.

Soup's letter was the second E.

Mine was the only N.

Mrs. Gooberman, our Sunday School teacher, always separated Soup and me, for some reason.

But she liked us enough to call us Holy Terrors, which meant she also liked dogs.

So, this time, to be extra helpful, I made sure not to stand at Soup's left.

Besides, I didn't want to march in last, so I took the middle . . . to please Mrs. Gooberman.

We spelled our three Easter words:
HE IS RINSE

The choir had to stop singing, and the other grown-ups also were laughing (except for my mother, who tried to duck under the pew).

Mrs. Gooberman yanked me (not very gently) to the end, stubbed her bunion toe, and mentioned *God.*

Then we kids sat down, and Mrs. Gooberman sneaked away to take two more Anacin and consider retirement.

I liked reading the Bible story.

It was all about lambs.

I guess they forgot to put in the rabbits.

* * *

After church wheezed to a tired halt,
Papa told our minister that we'd see
him again soon . . . at Christmas.

Mama pinched him.
Not the parson. She pinched Papa.

We all went home.
Soup's family, the Vinsons, arrived.
Bucky, the baby bunny, came too.
Papa and Mr. Vinson shared a cider
jug that had survived through a hard
winter without freezing.
They called it Sunday Cheer.
Soup put some ice in a bucket and
soaked one foot until it didn't turn blue.
It was purple.
Then, as Soup announced that we
had an Easter joke, we showed
everyone our feet.

Soup's foot was purple.
Mine was orange.

My mother sighed.
"*Why,*" she asked, "can't you be like normal children and dye *eggs*?"

"What else have you dyed?" Soup's mother asked, almost as if she hoped it wasn't the cat.

"We'll show you," we said.

Soup and I made everyone come to the barn to see if they'd find our hidden eggs.

Bucky came too.
We all walked.
Bucky hopped.

But, as we stopped inside our barn, Bucky kept going.

Up he jumped on a box, onto a barrel, and then up on another box.

From there to the shelf.

Soup whispered, "Golly, I hope Bucky doesn't go too close to the . . . *you know what.*"

But he did.

Bucky hid behind the large bushel basket.

The basket moved!

"Quick," said Soup, "we've got to stop him."

Both of us rushed forward.

Too late!

Good old Bucky kicked the basket, and over it spilled.

I saw it tilt.

"Catch the eggs," yelled Soup.

Out rolled the Easter eggs.

Down they fell.

Two green eggs.

Two purple.
Two blue.
Two red.
Two yellow.
And one orange.
All eleven landed on our heads, turning Soup and me a messy yellow and a sticky white.
The eggs had turned rotten and smelled awful.

The basket also landed on our heads, and I couldn't see.
It was one Peck in a bushel.

All we could hear was laughter.
And then our families started to sing:

"In your Easter bonnet,
With all the spills upon it . . ."

As we cuffed off the basket, I looked at Soup, and he looked back at me.

What a mess we were . . . covered with eleven busted eggs.

Soup grinned at me.

"Rob," he said, "*now* I remember why our mothers boiled the water."

"Why?" I asked, wiping egg yolks from my eyes. "Tell me."

"Easter eggs," said Soup, "have to be *hard-boiled*. So they won't break!"

Bucky the bunny jumped down from the shelf and licked egg off our faces.

He wasn't singing "Easter Parade."

Just smiling.

"Rob," said Soup, "the yolks are on *us*."